Night Mission

Seven WWII Era Stories

By Clive Lodge

These stories evoke an age gone by — and its values

Dedicated to: Nick Lodge

Also to Gerard, Michael and Catherine Hughes and Cedric Lodge.

Thanks to: Anne Coates for proof reading.

Cover design by Cooper Johnson Limited

© Lesley Lodge, 2014

All rights reserved. No part of this book may be reprinted or reproduced or utilized in any form or by any electronic, mechanical or other means now known or hereafter invented, including photocopying and recording or in any information storage or retrieval system without permission.

Contents

Foreword

Night Mission   Page 1

The Tunnel   Page 6

The Legacy   Page 13

There's No Scar Now   Page 17

Something She Said   Page 26

The Lucky Man   Page 29

A Question of Colour   Page 33

About the Author   Page 37

About the Editor   Page 37

Night Mission Beer   Page 38

Foreword

Most of these stories were written in the 1970s but based on the author's experiences in World War II, seen at times through the lens of a later decade. I found them in 2014, dusty - but typed up ready for a submission to publishers that never happened, languishing in the attic.

Clive Lodge – my father – was born in 1909. He joined the RAF voluntarily and served mainly as a navigator with the rank of flight lieutenant. He usually flew Beaufighters, but like many people he had a deep affection for the Spitfire. Clive's active service was with night-fighters – the setting for the short story *Night Mission*.

The Tunnel, by contrast, is set in peacetime, some years after the war but the writing clearly reveals how Clive was haunted by unpunished atrocities of war.

Clive's stories are very much of their time and they reflect the thinking and values of those years. *Something She Said*, for example, is about physical passion but the attitude towards premarital sex revealed by the first person narrator – and therefore the logic of its twist – would be almost incomprehensible to, say, today's teenagers in the UK.

There's No Scar Now – with its gripping opener "I killed John James Beresford" is set in Kent and draws on Clive's experience in the Home Guard before he enlisted in the RAF.

In all seven of these stories the detail and atmosphere evoked will take you back to those days.

Lesley Lodge
www.lesleylodge.co.uk

Night Mission

Night-fighting – and waiting. Geoff and I worked out on one occasion that the chance we had of doing anything spectacular arose just once per year. Our fallacious reasoning went roughly like this: of 365 nights in the year, we were on leave for 21, leaving 344. We, in "B" Flight, shared operational flying with "A" Flight, so the nights available were reduced to 172. Bad weather and U/S aircraft reduces to 80. Enemy activity in the area took place on average about one in eight nights, leaving ten possible nights. In "B" Flight we had ten crews taking first readiness in turn, so that we would be down to a chance of being on first readiness with a serviceable aircraft in good weather conditions with enemy aircraft in the area just *one* night a year.

This was that night.

I had already tired of playing poker and the dispersal hut was becoming increasingly smoky. Tension and boredom hung heavy in the air and when Lofty started his stupid word game I really gave up. Of all the puerile amusements resorted to, this was the limit. The idea was to think up a word that could meaningfully be dismantled from either end, one letter at a time, the most letters discarded being the winning word. He started with "uphill – Phill – hill – ill" and I struggled off my bunk and made for the door. It was 2:30 am.
  "Just going out for a bit of air, Geoff," I told my pilot. "I'll be within a few yards."
  " 'K", he answered. He was never much of a conversationalist and I could see he was preoccupied with his cards – he had a full house. I lumbered over to the door. We were, of course, all in full flying gear, which included, in my case, parachute harness, helmet, gloves and – strapped to my left thigh, the Course Setting Computer. The lot. And movement was neither easy nor comfortable. Outside, I found a perfect night, dark as a coalhouse. No moon, and even the stars obscured by a thin layer of high-flying cloud.
  Like the others, I was wearing the very dark glasses issued to protect and encourage night vision. It took about 20 minutes in a well-lit room before you could see anything at all through them when you first put them on but after something like 45 minutes you could see well enough

to play cards. It took a full hour before maximum night vision was obtained and this could be lost in a flash of any chance light. I took the glasses off and felt much relief.

I could clearly see our Beaufighter standing partly out of its bay, straining it seemed to me, towards the start of runway 225. It looked powerful, menacing, deadly, ready to spring into the air in search of prey. It was. We had taken her up on Night-flying Test earlier, and everything was as ready and prepared as human wit, energy and training could make it. Our personal record for scrambling was three and a quarter minutes from first alarm to wheels up. Tonight, if the chance arose, we hoped to reduce this to two and a half minutes.

I was mentally running over – for the hundredth time – my navigator's cockpit drill, when I became aware of the drone of aircraft. I listened keenly. One of ours? It was a "Heavy", a bomber. It didn't sound quite right. Not the familiar and synchronised "whirr-whirr" of an invader, but not right. It had trouble of some sort, that would be it. No alert on so it must be a "Friendly", in distress. As if to confirm my thoughts, the runway lights came on and from the tower a green Very light went soaring upwards. With it went most of my night vision. The roar of engines got louder, now downwind of the runway. It was coming in! As we were a highly secret night-fighter station it could only mean a desperate situation. The Friendly probably had wounded on board, so they couldn't bail out. Or she was too low and couldn't make height and so shot-up she could not make her own or even one of the emergency landing bases…

I peered towards the sound, trying to penetrate the blackness of the night. Nothing. I knew what to expect: just a slight darkening of darkness itself, a dim smudge of shape. Suddenly I saw it but not where it should have been. It was not in the normal glide path but low. Good God. Too low – and now I could make out an ominous orangey-red dim glow from her port wing. At least one engine was already on fire. She could not make it.

I started to run or shamble at best speed, slowed by all my clobber, towards the boundary. I hadn't gone far when she hit. An appalling explosion and a brilliant flash. Sudden silence, a deathly hush. And then came the roar of flames leaping high in the sky. Any slight hope of getting anyone away from that crash alive rested, I knew, with me – the nearest person. I stumbled on towards the perimeter fence. Behind me, I heard the clamour of the crash wagon and ambulances starting on their way. A figure, moving very fast and coming, I guess from

Dispersal, suddenly overtook me and went straight through what must have been a well-known gap in the fence. I lumbered after it feeling, I must admit, some relief at not being alone any more.

Now the terrifying scene was clear and hope of getting anyone out that inferno was dispelled. She must have had undercart down for she was standing nearly on her nose, enveloped in flame from there to her tail.

It could only be a funeral pyre, unless some poor devil had been thrown clear on impact. Occasional explosions sent bits of flying metal from the heart of the flames. The other would-be rescuer came towards me. He had a bundle in his arms, half carrying and half dragging it – for even through the smoke and flames I could see something burning following him through the blazing grass.

"I've got one," he shouted.

I couldn't reply. Partly due to smoke, heat, inability to think but also for emotion. One saved! A miracle. I stumbled towards him with the idea of helping. At that moment one of the burning bomber's fuel tanks went up with a roll and an indescribable sheet of flame. In the strong light I saw to my utter horror that it was not one of the aircrew he had. It was a parachute, partly opened.

"There's another one for you back there," he yelled at me.

I grabbed hold of him and spun him round. I recognised a Corporal Instrument Basher from our ground crew. I think I might have disgraced my commission by hitting him but just then the ammo in the bomber started to explode and the air was full of flying bullets and cartridge cases flying around without aim or objective but left right and overhead.

"Get down!" I shouted and I gave him a shove.

I was about to follow him when I heard above or through the noise the unmistakable sound of the scramble alarm. So I crouched down low and made my top speed – a speed encouraged by flying bullets – back through the fence and to our Beaufighter.

Geoff was already climbing in, up forward and, with practised effort and a few bruises, I clambered to my place aft. The well-rehearsed precision of a scramble take-off followed and – while I was still strapping myself in – the surge of acceleration came as Geoff took full advantage of the ready-warmed engines to swing straight onto the runway and into full power. My main job during take-off was to keep a sharp lookout astern and above for possible low-level enemy attack at this most vulnerable time, a time much favoured by the enemy. From their point of view – and understandably so – the rear of a Beaufighter was a much better proposition than the front where four canons and six machine guns would surely greet them. This time things were complicated by the glare from the burning aircraft and the pall of smoke above it, both now fast receding. I was vaguely aware of Geoff changing channels from flying control to ground control who gave his orders to make Angels Seven (7000 feet) and go on orbital patrol. It was clear that we were to intercept any attack that might be made by intruders drawn to the scene by the fire, which was still visible below, just a spot of light on a carpet of inky blackness.

Well, we kept up patrol for two hours without any real action. We were twice elected by control on to two unidentifieds and made – more by luck than judgement – good interception, coming in below and astern and identifying a Lancaster each time. We reported in both cases the height, course magnetic and speed in a coded message so that from then on they would be monitored and finally led to base. Neither of them ever knew, I'm sure, that they had the most powerful airborne fighter armament of the time just 800 feet under their tails.

Dawn's eerie light – it *was* eerie – grew stronger, pinpointing us whilst the earth below was still secure in darkness. We were glad to be recalled, especially as our patrol was within three and a half minutes flying time from an M.E. 109 base and at that time the advantage would have been theirs... The day boys, the Spitfires and Hurricanes, would have taken over by now and we were not long in landing and getting up to the Mess for the traditional night flying supper. The rest of the flight came in shortly after us and conversation turned to the pranged bomber incident. Shorty was, of course, in possession of the full story and it was from him that I heard that my Corporal Instrument Basher was dead.

"How the hell did that happen?" I asked. I had told no one of my own useless rescue effort.

"Well," said Shorty, "he was found by the crash wagon people, quite close to the prang and apparently the ammo was going off and he got hit in the throat by tracer bullet. Nasty. He was obviously going towards the aircraft to lend a hand. Jolly good show."

The talk switched to our own trip. One did not dwell for long on fatal prangs.

***

We started our two rest days. Normally the first day was given up to sleeping and eating and the second day to a blitz on the town for a meal, drinks and whatever the place offered but this time the second day was a Sunday and the town would not be too lively. So when the CO asked for a bit of support for the church parade several of us went along. What was special about it was that the padre had in mind incorporating a bit of a service for those in the prang.

It was a pleasant enough morning with a fresh breeze blowing – blowing enough to blow away most of the Padre's words – from where I was. So only the occasional parts of his sermon reached me and I lost some of those as my mind was wandering as usual.

"… None of us knows when he or she might be called upon for a supreme effort…"

A squadron of starlings took off from the top of number two hanger, in a rather ragged formation I thought, making a climbing turn to port, causing the starboard winger to lose his place. He soon made it up by – I suppose – increasing his revs a bit. I wondered idly how birds choose their positions in flight. Did they, for instance, have a bird NCO with no knowledge of his egg-laying mother to line them? "Nah, then, you ugly lot of birds, get fell in. Weakest on the left, strongest on the right…."

My thoughts were disturbed by another change of wind. The padre was saying "… And so he died, facing into danger. One of whom we are proud. A real hero. Let us pray."

Yes, I thought, why not? I'll go along with that.

So we prayed.

The Tunnel

Usually, I like writing stories. A writer has such great power. He or she can make any types of characters at will and make them perform in any way that pleases or amuses. Or create a fat, gross, squint-eyed one-toothed one-legged man who has such powerful sex appeal that no woman can resist his crude advances – then have him murdered, commit suicide or live happily. In short, the writer can do what he likes – usually.

This time, this story, is different. The tables have turned and I am at the mercy and the will of the characters. People I have neither met nor heard of. People who have invaded my dreams, turning them into nightmares, so long and so often that I've decided to write down what I'm directed. It's my effort to clear my mind and free myself of this wretched theme once and for all - if possible.

I've searched so many likely places but I've found no trace of the mountain or the village that come to me in my dreams so often. Some places have had a similarity in some respects – obviously this must be so – but nowhere have I located such a site as to make me think, "at last, here it is".

This story is one that I would rather leave untold. But there seems to be someone, some thing, which will give me no rest until I make note of the affair. The following is not my story. Not my characters. Not my conversations. Not my thoughts. I simply record it as directed, as seen and heard in the long restless hours many a night.

***

It was early spring in what I feel must be about 1970 that Peter Langford and his wife Anna came to the little village of St Michel-la-Roche, a small oasis of humanity set high in the clean-scented mountains about 1200 metres above sea level and, thus, Peter thought, about 40 kilometres from the sea. The road leading up to it had been so winding, with so many U-turns and hairpin bends that it was difficult to work out how far it would be should the proverbial crow take off from the mountain and glide to the sea.

Peter and Anna were making a leisurely boat trip along the Cote d'Azur and were on the third week of their charter. Perfect weather had been marred only once by the fierce but short-lived mistral and to make a change from the heat they pointed the nose of a hired Peugeot into the mountains. After climbing steadily, turning and swerving all the way, they found that the road entered into a very short tunnel that was carved into the actual rock. Darkness changed abruptly into dazzling light. They found themselves in the central square of the village of St Michel-laRoche.

Tucked away in hidden folds of the mountains, the little village faced mainly to the south. Several of the houses were quite literally built into the rock of the mountain itself. Some had an entrance on two or even three floors. The buildings were huddled together as though for company, gaining some protection from both the winds in winter and the sun in summer. When Peter and Anna arrived it was nearly noon and the little square was a mosaic of light and shade, of heat and cold. In the centre stood a stone fountain, with cold, clear mountain water flowing from – of all things – the mouth of a carved dolphin into a large circular base that looked set to overflow. The water, though, drained away through two troughs to an underground drain. From there it cascaded down the valley.

On the southern valley side was a cafe bar. Its weathered lettering proclaimed it to be the Bar du Vallon. It had magnificent views to the south, looking down the forest-clad valley. Next to this was a kind of village general store, its main display consisting of fruit and vegetables overflowing from boxes, bags, packages and bunches into the square. Across the square, on the mountainside, was a tiny but solid looking church. By the side of the church an unpretentious looking restaurant endeavoured to catch the eye of any passing stranger by means of a glass sign with the legend "Coq d'Or". The coq in question was a painted caricature of a bird, looking more like a tired vulture than a cock bird. It had one leg and most of the tail feathers missing.

Peter and Anna parked the Peugeot in the square and strolled along the road a little further.

"Let's just see round this corner," said Peter, "then we'll have a drink, lunch, explore a bit and return to the coast in time for dinner. How does that sound?"

"Fine," said Anna "especially the lunch bit."

They walked on through the square, along the road, by the side of a single block of white marble, which carried no lettering to indicate its purpose but had a small vase on the top with a spray of Mimosa in it. A little further along they came to a second, small tunnel. It was obvious that the only way in or out of the village must be through one or other of the two tunnels.

Anna was intrigued.

"How do you suppose they knew this sort of shelf in the valley was here when they started digging tunnels?" she asked.

"Perhaps," said Peter "they started from here and dug their way out into the world. Perhaps life started here?"

"Don't be silly," Anna said. "Let's have that drink and ask someone. Is your French up to it do you think? What's the French for tunnel?"

"That's an easy one," Peter answered, "it's *tunnel*."

They made their way to the Bar du Vallon and went inside. Peter was impressed by the habit the French had of acknowledging the existence of other humans. In the current circumstances, he thought, it made a pleasant change from the preferred habit of the English: looking straight through other customers as though they simply didn't exist.

"*M'sieurs,*" he said with a nod of his head to the four customers seated at the table.

"*Monsieur, Madame,*" came the reply. Strange how they always greet the male first. Something to do, no doubt, he thought, with the Revolution.

The little bar was a carbon copy of countless others. Bare floor, bare tables – to facilitate the essential breadcrumb clearing, he thought. Opposite the entrance, the usual small bar, with a couple of stools in front. Behind the bar, rows of multicoloured liquids and syrups. A large mirror doubled the number of bottles and supported the obligatory sign dealing with "L'Ivresse" and sale of alcohol to the under-aged. Also, behind the bar the usual coffee making machine quietly hissing away, ever ready to produce noise, steam, boiling water and, eventually, excellent coffee. Underneath it was the drawer into which the coffee grouts, after use, were emptied. Neither Peter not Anna had ever seen one of those drawers emptied. And why a drawer, they had often wondered and then again, why not?

As they seated themselves, the Patron turned from caressing the coffee machine. He was quite old, with wrinkled skin and eyes that seemed full of pain. Humourless. Tired.

"*M'sieur?*" A slight raising of the thin white eyebrows indicated that he was ready to receive notice of his new customers' requirements.

"*Une bierre, un vin blanc, s'il vous plait,*" Peter ordered.

He turned to look round the small room, paying particular attention to the four other men at their table in the corner. They were, he noted, all elderly. Difficult to judge their actual ages. They all wore similar flat caps set level on their heads. They all wore rough jackets. Two had woollen scarves draped round their necks, in spite of the sunshine outside. Perhaps they felt the chill of the mountain air when they went on their way. Three were half-heartedly playing a card game of some sort, whilst the fourth was reading what appeared to be the local paper. Or was he? Peter thought he caught him looking over the paper more than at it. It didn't worry him unduly though – Anna often caused something of a stir amongst men of all ages. On the table in front of them was a carafe of water and four glasses with the milky white medicine-tasting Pernod.

The Patron emerged from behind his bar bearing the drinks on a tray, and with him came a shadow over the Langfords' holiday. He was very thin and perhaps a little tall; the most noticeable thing about him was his way of walking. He seemed to stagger. So unsteady was he on his legs that he moved with a fast stumbling step as though the tray held far in front of him was constantly about to fall. It seemed obvious that he had been injured in some way.

He placed the drinks on the table.

"English?" he asked.

"Yes," replied Peter and Anna, together.

"You speak English?" continued Peter.

"A little. Enough."

"Oh good," said Peter, "my French is not too good, unless I have plenty of time to think. My wife is curious about the two entrances, the two tunnels, and wonders how the village came to be here."

"*Alors, monsieur*, a long time ago this coast was raided by everyone for miles around and this village became a sort of natural fort. The tunnel entrance was easy to defend, there was plenty of water, and all who could gathered here when plunderers landed."

"Ah, that explains it, " said Peter. "Thank you."

"But," said Anna, "would they not be starved out in time? And what would happen if the roads were blocked by snow or rocks?"

The patron shrugged his shoulders.

"*N'importe*," he said, "there is a third way out in an emergency but is difficult and known only to the *Maquis*. It is a long but small third tunnel."

"The *Maquis*? French Resistance?" Peter asked, surprised, "they were here then? Do you mean you were occupied? You had the Germans here during the war?"

The patron's manner changed abruptly. His lips tightened into thin lines.

"*Mon Dieu*," he said, "*Mon Dieu,* yes they were here. Oh yes. I'm waiting for them to come again. One of them. One would do."

He turned abruptly, muttering in French and, reaching the bar, he took down a spare bottle of Pastis, picked up a glass and made it to the door by the bar, into the private quarters. At the door he paused, looking towards the group of regulars at the table.

"Charles!" he said – and vanished through the door.

The man who had been reading the paper put it aside and walked to the bar without a word. It was obviously an oft-rehearsed manoeuvre. He made himself a glass of Pastis and put it on a tray with an uncorked bottle of beer and a glass of wine. He took it to the table where Peter and Anna were finishing their drinks.

"*Permettez moi?*" he said. "Will you allow me to join you? And please have a drink with me. I feel I should explain to you that Axcel, le Patron, does not mean to be abrupt. He becomes excited at times. With some reason."

He raised his glass.

"*Santé* – or as you would say, cheers."

Peter and Anna raised their glasses in acknowledgement.

"Is it his accident?" asked Anna. "I mean, I thought perhaps he has had a bad accident? The way he walks…" Her voice died away with embarrassment.

"Yes, " said Charles, "it was like this: during the occupation the Germans had a small SS group established here. They took over the Coq d'Or for their headquarters. Unknown to them, the local resistance, the *maquis*, had a base here. Next door, as it were, in this *Auberge*. The mountain road on its way north here winds up and down and roundabout and actually passes quite close by the other side of this mountain. By the route that Axcel mentioned, the Maquis could see a German vehicle or convoy leave here going north and although on foot they could get across the mountain, shoot them up and return here where they showed themselves for an alibi. Well, the German commander, a major, got more and more furious with the constant losses and his temper erupted one day. A patrol wagon came into the square one hot afternoon and they had with them tied up little Christot, Axcel's boy, just ten years old. They had found him in the forest and they produced half a loaf and a piece of cheese they had found on him. It was his lunch and he had gone into the forest to check the snares he had set. Food was short in those days you must understand. The Germans were convinced he was taking food to the *Maquis*. They began beating the boy, futilely hoping to get information out of him. Axcel ran to his aid. A large German corporal swinging his rifle like a club struck Axcel across the legs, breaking both of them. He lay there in agony while the SS major drew his Mauser pistol and shot the boy dead. They then got a can of petrol from the armoured car poured over the boy and set fire to it. Yes that's what they did. Just where the stone is in the square."

Charles fell silent.

"Horrible," whispered Anna, her face taut with emotion.

"Good God! How appalling," said Peter, "poor man, no wonder he went off. We shouldn't have raised the subject. If only we'd known…"

"It's alright," said Charles, "it's not your fault. It happens often in the season."

"What happened afterwards?" Peter asked. "Was the SS man tried by the courts?"

"No," said Charles. "Axcel was carted off to prison, without medical attention. Shortly afterwards the Allies were here and the Germans had fled. Axcel was rescued and taken to hospital but as you have seen too late to do more than a rough job on his legs. The SS major escaped, although the *Maquis* were out to get him. He swore he would find out how the *Maquis* got their information round the mountain, even if he had to come back one day. That is what Axcel – and we – are waiting for. Five of us. Still waiting."

Peter looked at Anna and saw that she was somewhat distressed, disturbed by this unexpected and unwelcome intrusion into what was supposed to be a carefree, light-hearted holiday jaunt into the mountains. He stood up and held out his hand to Charles. "Terribly sorry," he said "our condolences to *Monsieur* Axcel and – *au revoir.*"

He took Anna by the arm and led her out into the square. She looked round and was struck by the grim forbidding rock faced buildings, the ominous shadows. She looked towards the car and saw an armoured truck with a large black cross painted on it. Three children, squatting on the ground became three SS men in coal bucket helmets and field grey uniforms, crouching over a machine gun. The mountain breeze had the icy breath of death in it. She shuddered and lent heavily on her husband.

"Steady, old girl," he said, "into the car and let's get the hell out of here and down to the sunshine and the beaches."

As they wound their way down the twisting road, their ears painfully popping from time to time as they reduced their altitude he tried to jolly Anna into a better humour.

"Those funny men, you know, Anna, were not really *Maquis* fellows – they are the gnomes of Zürich on holiday." No response. He tried again. "Honestly darling they're not really old men, they are about 25 years old. Actually they just look old after roaming over the mountains looking for girlfriends."

"Peter."

"Yes dear?"

"SHUT UP!"

They continued in a silent gloomy mood until at last they reach their boat and there, with much to do and warm sunshine, the tragedy of the mountains receded from their minds. It did not return again until, the holiday over, they were back at their house in Sunbury. They had spent much of their last holiday week looking for a flat or apartment anywhere on the Cote d'Azur. Without success and they had arranged for a weekly publication the *Bord de la Mer Week End* which contained many adverts and property office to be posted from time to time. It was in the news review of this paper some ten weeks after their return to England that they found the following news item roughly translated as:

"Police appeal for information

The badly burned body found in mysterious circumstances in the square at St Michel la-Roche has been identified as Otto Muller, of West Germany aged about 60 years. Nothing further of his movements on the night of his death is known. It is certain that he entered the Bar du Vallon, and four of the regular customers have testified that he left the bar about 8 pm and drove off in a black Mercedes. How he came to return to the village, how he met his terrible death and why no one in the village saw or heard the fire is puzzling police who are urgently appealing for anyone with information regarding M Muller's movements on the night in question to come forward."

Peter looked at Anna as they finished reading. A look of understanding showed in her eyes. "Yes, I guess he came back," said Peter.

The Legacy

The farm worked by Dave's father was on the edge of the village, so that the front door of the farmhouse, so to speak, opened not on to a lane but into a road which was built up on the other side by development and in-filling until the planners had called a halt at the frontier with agriculture. By contrast, the back of the farmhouse opened onto the usual clutter of farm impediments, yard, mud, barns, mud, milking parlour – and mud. Beyond, the land gently undulated in a typical English countryside way, with occasional copses on the small hills and a few giant oaks in the centres of pastures where the milk herd grazed. From the highest point the land sloped gradually down to the small stream that wandered leisurely along through the village on its way to the sea.

It was Thirty Acre field that interested Dave more than any other part of the farm. At just over fifteen years old, he did his fair share at every activity and didn't, therefore, have much spare time. But when he was free and the weather was fair, he would walk endlessly around Thirty Acre field, especially near the northern edge where a symmetrically rounded small hill proclaimed itself a barrow or some man-made ancient relic. Perhaps a burial ground? An old castle? Fort? Village? Perhaps a lost city lay under Thirty Acre?

Dave's father, Les Johnson, had no interest in such matters. Many a time he reasoned with Dave on this subject.

"A lost city," he said, "if found, would only mean a lost harvest to me. And as for buried treasure, why I get buried treasure up from the earth with every crop. That's the way to earn your living, son. No good hoping for it to jump out of the earth at your feet."

But Dave remained unconvinced. His main driving force – if youthful optimism can be so-called – came from the finding, over the years, of a total of seven coins, five of which were of Roman origin and two so worn and tarnished as to be indecipherable but thought to be Anglo-Saxon. They had all been found in Thirty Acre.

Now, for the reasons already mentioned, Dave's father would not buy for him nor allow him to borrow the metal detector that Dave mentioned at every available opportunity. There the matter might well have rested had Dave not, on his way home from school, come across a water company employee searching for an unrecorded water pipe. He was using divining rods and Dave was fascinated. By endless questioning he extracted as much information as the unfortunate diviner had about their use and he hurried home in great excitement.

In the workshop at the farm, where very occasional attempts were made to service the farm machinery, Dave soon found a length of metal rod and from this he made two lengths with right-angled "handles" bent into them. Each was 24 inches long. With one in each hand held close and steady to his body with the rods extended forward and parallel, he started practising. At first he was disappointed. Nothing seemed to work and when he did get a movement over a metal object, he had to admit to himself that he had aided and even started the movement. After a few days, however, he became fairly efficient and could locate coins hidden under sacks and leaves about four out of five times.

His father watched these antics without enthusiasm but became mildly impressed as Dave's efficiency increased.

"What do you expect to come from all this waste of time, son?" he asked.

Dave had an instant answer.

"Somewhere, and maybe in Thirty Acre, there is buried treasure waiting for someone to find. A sort of legacy from former times. Mr Jackson, our history teacher, says that the Earth is covered with relics from previous people and he says that some of the things they left behind are a sort of legacy to whoever finds them – but only for the benefit of everyone. He says every nation leaves something behind for others to find. And if it's there, I'll find it. Dad, Thirty Acre has just been ploughed – it won't do any harm if I go over it, just walking along, will it?"

"No," said his father, "it won't do any harm. But the thing is, what darn good will it do? You do your jobs first. You can go after that. You ought to pay more attention to living in this time and not hoping for a handout from the past."

Dave took this as permission to proceed and for several days when school, homework, farm work and weather permitted, he was out walking slowly and methodically along the ploughed furrows in Thirty Acre. His rewards were meagre. Several rusty old horseshoes, a few old iron bolts fallen from machinery some long time ago and little else. Until, that is, late on a Friday evening when near the top of the rising slope the rods crossed in front of him with a vigour and force he had never felt before. He searched backwards and forwards crossing and re-crossing the same place and always with the same incredibly strong indication of some strange force, something that set his heart pounding from excitement. This was real. No need to think that he might have imagined it! He gripped the rods more tightly but the pull was strong and still the rods swung together and crossed each other to lie across his chest. From his hours of practice, he knew that vertically below the point where the rods crossed lay the source of the as yet unknown energy.

He marked out the area by scraping his foot across and along the furrows making a roughly square yard. Using one of the divining rods as a probe, he felt something solid at the extreme depth, that is about two feet below the bottom of the furrow. It was by now growing dark and reluctantly he decided to leave the site. He made his way home with suppressed excitement.

"I'll surprise them," he thought, "tomorrow, I'll dig it up. I'll show them what I mean by a legacy from former times. What if it's gold treasure? Or jewels? Or coins? What should I do with it?"

He thought perhaps if possible he would try to keep some of it hidden and let "them" see the rest. He wasn't quite sure who "they" would be but of course his dad would know what to do and after all it was his land. But keeping a bit for himself, well, could that be so very wrong? Who found it anyway?

Saturday morning dawned bright and clear and his excitement over his unusually hurried breakfast caused his mother to ask him what it was all about.

"It's nothing," he said as thousands of young boys had answered similar questions in the past.

"Nothing at all. Just that I may have found a coin in a Thirty Acre. But it's deep down and I'm going to dig it up. Could I have some sandwiches please for lunch? And if Linda calls this afternoon and I'm not back will you tell her where I am please?"

"Alright," his mother agreed.

Linda was, she thought, a very nice girl and though of course it was far too early for serious thoughts she was vaguely pleased at her son's choice of girlfriend. So she was quite happy when Linda called at the farm just after lunch.

"Dave's fooling around with those rod things again, Linda," she said "and he hopes you will go to meet him in Thirty Acre. He's up to something – thinks he's found a legacy of gold treasure! Some hopes!

That field's been deep ploughed 20 times to my knowledge and nothing but good crops has ever come out of it."

Linda smiled and set off across the home pasture. It was a warm and sunny afternoon and she enjoyed the stroll across the meadow, slowing down a bit as she climbed the gentle slope that led to the top of Thirty Acre.

She was near the top when it happened. There seem to be a heavy thud on the ground and then she found herself lying on that ground, rather breathless and dazed. After a while she struggled to her feet, a little unsteady and bewildered but otherwise unharmed. There was a sudden swishing the air as a gold coloured piece of metal landed with a clunk in the grass at her feet.

She still has that piece of metal to this day. It is a treasured possession although it is not made of gold and the scrap of writing on it is not Roman or old English but German. Even so, the meaning is pretty clear. *Explosiv* it says. And it is the only thing she has left a reminder of Dave and his legacy from a former age.

There's No Scar Now

The coroner's verdict on the death of John James Beresford was one of "murder by person or persons unknown". This was recorded on 15 October, 1940. Later, in the December, the file was amended to "murder by Hans Bleucher, of German nationality". And then marked "closed" and sent to Records. Both these findings were incorrect.

I killed John James Beresford.

I let Hans Bleucher take the blame. Hans Bleucher, who not only admitted the killing but was proud of it and was executed for it or for being a spy in due course. I don't know which of these two crimes led to the death penalty and certainly to him it matters not. Spy he certainly was. Murderer he was not.

So after some 40 years and before it is too late, I feel that the time has come for me to put the record straight. That someone else was charged with taking the human life that in fact I had taken – this has not disturbed me. I have always slept well. But reading recently a book dealing with events of that time, a book that seemed to have several factual errors in it, I feel that as no one else knows the facts, it'll be just as well to put the record straight.

First, although no one could prove anything, I must state that any resemblance to living persons is coincidental and this story has no connection with any living person – or any dead one, come to that. And the town of Marbay did not exist at the time mentioned. That should give me some cover...

***

It was on 15 September, 1940, in the south-east corner of England – the frontline. The Battle of Britain, which was also the Battle *for* Britain, was reaching its climax, although we didn't know that at the time. Hitler was about to invade, air raids were constant and terrifying, the armed forces awaiting the might of German power were pitiful in their number and equipment. I was a member of the Home Guard, a one-time Local Defence Volunteer, and worked in local government at Marbay, on the Kent coast. I'd recently been transferred there from London as most of the Marbay staff had been taken into the Services.

I was residing on a bed, breakfast and evening meal basis with a Mr and Mrs Pearson in their small semi-bungalow on the outskirts of the town. Mr Pearson was, I understood, connected with the police and/or the Home Office in some way, his exact duties unknown to me. Too many questions were not encouraged in those days but whatever it was he did, it meant he had to be away on night duty quite often and he and Mrs Pearson were glad to have me around. She was extremely nervous, especially at night and during raids, and she dreaded the occasional nights when my night-time cliff-top patrols coincided with Mr Pearson's night duty.

It was a night when Brian – Mr Pearson – was on night duty that the trouble started. It had been a day of warnings, heavy raids, bombs, fighters, machine gunning, vapour trails, survivors, parachutes, sirens, fires, tragedies and – all too rarely – a touch of humour. An example of the latter occurred that Sunday afternoon when I was at home. The warning went and before long the sky was filled with bombers and fighters and the now customary dogfights taking place everywhere. I usually stayed out to watch; there was no shelter and one could see possible danger approaching.

The danger this time was a German bomber, a Dornier, coming towards the bungalow, very low down. He was hugging the ground to escape the attentions of an attacking fighter, apparently successfully for the Hurricane broke off the attack. Probably out of ammunition. I could see that the bomber would come directly over us, flying straight and level with both engines going. So I grabbed my rifle, shoved in a clip, put a round up the breech and took careful sight on him, starting at the tail and traversing the pencil-like fuselage to a deflection of about five degrees ahead of him. I let him have the well-known "five rounds rapid".

God knows where the last bullet went, for my arm was jerked round by a furious and frightened Mrs Pearson, screaming.

"Stop! Stop! You fool, you'll make him angry!"

A strange view of warfare. It appeared she thought the bomber would make a circle and return to drop his bomb load on the impudent person who dared to fire at him with his little rifle... I believe the bomber crashed into the sea off Marbay a few minutes later. But I don't claim it as mine...

That night I came off duty just before 10 pm and made my way home via the local pub where I had a couple of pints in lieu of supper. Mrs Pearson seemed glad to see me and said she would be off to her bed, now that there was someone in the house and there was no alert on. Accordingly away she went. I listened briefly to the radio, then went up to my room, which was next to the Pearsons' room and turned in, grateful for a bit of peace and quiet. As usual, I left my uniform, torch and rifle handy. An undisturbed night was unusual and it was as well to be as prepared as possible for heaven knew what.

Sure enough, the sirens went off about 4 am. Having no shelter to go to, the simplest thing was to stay put and be fatalistic. If one could.

It wasn't long before the droning whirr-whirr, the well-known unsynchronised engine sound of an enemy aircraft, was heard. It grew steadily louder, nearer. My ears felt as though they were standing up like a rabbit's, listening for tell-tale noises: bomb doors opening, the scream of falling bombs, gun-fire, anything. But they were not prepared for what followed. Suddenly there was a very heavy thump or our roof, just above my head, and a crash on the ceiling. Some plaster showered down. They were seconds of breath-catching silence, broken only by the sound of the aircraft fading away. Then came a slow, sinister scraping, dragging, rustling noise as though something – or *someone*? – was sliding down the roof. There was a final thud and then complete and utter silence.

A cry of terror came from Mrs Pearson in the next room.

"Mr Richards, oh, Mr Richards, come quickly, *what* is it?"

I snapped out of my spellbound state, slid out of bed, opened my door and called to her.

"Keep quiet, for heaven's sake, don't make a sound. It's all right. I'll be with you in a minute."

"What was it? What shall I do?" She was sobbing now, ignoring my instructions.

"Stay where you are and keep quiet for God's sake." I practically hissed.

"Oh my God," she said, "they've come. It's the invasion. What will they do to us?"

She was nearly screaming now.

"Don't leave me… You can't go. You mustn't go. I'll be left alone at their mercy…"

Her voice trailed away.

"Now listen," I said, "I *must* find out what is happening. It might be one of our night fighters bailed out needing help."

I didn't tell her that it might also be a German paratrooper, armed to the teeth with sub-machine gun, hand grenades etc. Or – and a chill went up my spine at the thought – a landmine dropped by parachute with perhaps a delayed action fuse…

In any case, it was obvious that I had to find out. It wasn't a case of heroics but of common sense. I slipped back to my room, pulled on slacks and a dark sweater, stepped into my slippers and grabbed my rifle. I put in a clip of bullets and silently worked the bolt to put one up the spout. Then I soft-footed it down the stairs. There were no lights on, the black-out was still up and it was of course as black as possible – which suited me. I knew the way and I wanted to preserve my night vision for outside use.

My thoughts went racing ahead, thinking of the possibilities and the probabilities. What could have caused the heavy thud on the tiles, the scraping, rustling sound? Obviously it had come from above. Too heavy to be a falling bird – and what would be flying around at night? An owl? Not heavy enough. Was it a coincidence that an aircraft was passing overhead? No, for sure that had something to do with it. A lone aircraft was not likely to be part of an invasion force… Surely Hitler would send rather more than one aircraft. A parachutist? A spy? Or the dreaded landmine?

I began to favour the spy theory. In any case I had to find out. Right. So out we go. Front door? No. It creaked every time and would be heard yards away. Back door? No. It opened onto a gravel path and just one step would give me away. Side door? Yes. This opened onto a small patio with the lawn right at the edge and shrubs for cover nearby. Gently I eased the door open, inch by inch. Outside, it seemed fairly light by comparison with the blackness of the interior. I peered round, saw nothing unusual, nothing moving. I heard nothing. Now to scout around.

I edged my feet out of my slippers. I could move as silently as a ghost without them, feeling each footstep gingerly before putting weight on it. Slow but sure. My hastily conceived plan was to get several yards away from the house, into the cover of the shrubs and background darkness and make a detour to see if I could locate the parachute – or whatever or whoever had come down. I hoped I might see it silhouetted against the light-coloured walls of the house.

In the distance the rumble of anti-aircraft guns could be heard occasionally, coming from up the Thames. Probably after a mine-laying aircraft. Good God! Mine-layers! Could it be a mine dropped by parachute on us by mistake? Or deliberately jettisoned? Magnetic perhaps?

I was now working my way past a clump of rhododendrons by the gate in the hedge giving out onto the road. I froze. The gate was open, showing rather as a patch of less dark than as a gate. A dark shadowy figure suddenly and quietly filled the opening. It moved silently and came into the garden. It was a human of some sort, that much I could make out, and this was verified when it apparently stumbled over an obstruction of some kind. I could just make out a small dark lump showing against the likeness of the path. I was now within ten feet and holding my breath. Slowly I brought the muzzle of my rifle to bear on the figure, holding it level with my hips.

I was going to get myself a *spy*.

I couldn't think of the German for "Hands up!" and I thought if I used English my spy would know for sure I was his enemy. He would no doubt expect everyone to be his enemy but if I could confuse him, just for a split second, I would have a slight advantage. So in what I hoped was a firm, authoritative voice, I said, "Haute les Mains!"

And stepped forward.

The reaction of the figure was not quite what I expected. With a strange kind of growl it hurled itself at me. I was too surprised to fire but without knowingly instigating the movement, I drove the barrel of the rifle into the shape's middle. It made a noise between a groan, cough, a yell or a curse and doubled up. In a swift movement I stepped one side, slid my right hand from the stock to the barrel and using the rifle is a club brought it down hard on the base of the shape's head. The shape, now clearly a man, dropped as though poleaxed.

I looked quickly round, searching for any more of the enemy. There was no one. No sound. No sign of any further action. I wasn't expecting more than one person to be around, so I risked a dim light to look at the obstacle on the ground, in case it presented an immediate danger. It was a grey coloured waterproof canvas pack, with what looked like a shoulder strap, broken, as it was fastened but only one end. A bright piece of metal in one corner caught my eye and I looked closer. I knew it immediately. It was the top of a telescopic aerial. The box was a wireless set. Definitely, I'd got my spy!

I moved the small circle of light towards the figure on the ground. It lay face downwards and I turned it over to look at the face. With a shock, I realise that the head did not appear to turn with the body… I turned the head and it became clear that the neck was broken. At the same time a second shock sent my own head reeling. I recognised the face. It was that of old Mr Beresford. I knew him as something of a recluse who lived in a small bungalow a few yards along the road. I shone my torch over the rest of him. Dressing gown, pyjamas – a rather vivid purple colour, I noticed – and carpet slippers. Like me, I thought, he had come out into the road to see what, if anything, was going on. We had met once or twice that way before. I remember the last time we stood watching the bomb flashes in the direction of Canterbury. Possibly he had seen a parachute float down and had come to investigate? The thought struck me that had I challenged him in English he might not have reacted so violently. Perhaps hearing a foreign language of some sort he assumed I was an enemy and most courageously sprang instantly into the attack.

I felt terrible. I'd killed an innocent person. Still, it was a genuine mistake and he probably hadn't got long to go anyway. In the circumstances, the darkness, the war, the never strain we were all under... I realised I was making excuses for what I'd done. But what to do now? That was the question. Well, there were no witnesses and no help was needed or could serve any useful purpose. I lifted the body, surprised at how light it was, and carried it through the gate, across and along the road and laid it down by the wall of number 10. I checked the road for any possible witness but saw no one and I made my way back to the gate. I went to pick up the wireless set. It wasn't there – it was gone.

While my brain was spinning around trying to evaluate this new situation, the rising moan of the "All Clear" siren filled the air. I heard a slight noise behind me and started to turn but too late. The night sky exploded into a thousand coloured lights and I lost consciousness.

I came round slowly, taking some time to discover who I was, where I was, and why. I was lying on the path by the gate and my head hurt like hell. Already I could feel a lump at the base of my skull. I became aware also of a smarting pain under my chest on the left-hand side. Cautiously I looked around and was glad to find that I appeared to be alone. The sky seemed a bit brighter, partly due to clear skies and a rising moon. I picked myself up and made my way unsteadily into the house and put the hall light on. A quick look in the mirror showed no outward sign of the events of the last few minutes – or was it hours? A swift glance at my watch showed only some twenty minutes had passed since I went out. A thought struck me. Where was my assailant? And who was the? What if he had followed me in? My rifle!

"Oh my God!" I thought, "he's got that as well..."

I switched off the lights and went out again. I could not see very well now, after the light indoors.

"To hell with it."

I switched on my torch and went round to the gate. My rifle was lying on the grass verge, just about where I would have dropped it when slugged. Thankfully I picked it up and went back indoors.

"Mrs Pearson!" I shouted. "Mrs Pearson, are you all right?"

There was the sound of a bed creaking upstairs and then she appeared complete with dressing gown and curlers.

"What was it?" she asked, "you shouldn't have left me. I might have been killed in my bed…"

She went on and on until I stopped by suggesting a cup of tea. Magic words in those days. Any time, day or night, any situation, any emergency: a cup of tea seem to be the answer.

I went off to the bathroom and investigated my hurts. Yes there was a hell of a lump on the back of my head, but the skin was unbroken. Just below my ribs, my old sweater was torn and my pyjama jacket had a slit in it. Both were soaked in blood. I slipped them off, and found a three-inch cut on my stomach, just below the rib cage. It was not, I thought, a deep cut and it seemed that my stout leather belt, which kept my slacks up, was also slashed nearly in half and at the end of the cut, wedged in the buckle, was the tip of a knife blade that had broken off. So, I had been slugged and whilst on the ground a knife blow intended for my heart had been struck. I fixed a rough dressing and plaster on the wound, put my clothes and dressing gown back on and went downstairs. I needed that cup of tea.

My next move was to telephone my Home Guard HQ and tell them of the thump on the roof and that I had searched the area quickly and found nothing but I was quite positive that someone had landed, most likely an enemy agent from the hostile aircraft that are passed overhead at the time. I suggested they send help to search for the parachute that I was sure must be close by somewhere. Before I had finished my third cup of tea, the army had arrived. Like hounds after a fox they spread out searching and within minutes they had found the body on the pavement along the road and the parachute tucked under the garden shed.

Assuming the spy to be the assailant and that he had gone along the road in that direction, which led to the cliff-top, frantic calls were made and signals sent. Within an hour, my CO came through on the telephone to tell me they had captured the German who had walked straight into a hidden checkpoint on the cliff path. He also said that the German admitted his identity and not only did he admit to killing someone where he had landed but he was proud of it.

"A right cocky little Nazi bastard," was how the CO described him. "Said he was honoured to have killed at least one of the Fuhrer's enemies."

Apparently he wasn't the least bit frightened, but was sure that he would be freed within a couple of days by the invading forces. And he quite expected to be in London, dining at the Savoy within a week…

I also learned that my spy, as I still thought of him, was armed with a Mauser automatic, a knife and a weighted rubber cosh. He told the Intelligence people that he was interrupted by someone and coshed him, finishing him off with a knife, the blade of which broke at the tip. And examination of the body found that the cause of death was a broken neck, the result of a heavy blow from a very blunt instrument but, said the CO, there was no knife wound, only an abrasion on the stomach, though the dressing gown was torn and a button broken – which tallied with a broken knife blade. "So," he said, "we've got him either way – he'll be hanged for murder or be shot as a spy."

It was shortly after this that my call-up came and the next few weeks in the forces drove all thoughts out of my mind other than those needed for the day-to-day or minute by minute existence until my first leave – 48 hours – came in January. I returned then to Marbay. It was on this short visit that Mr Pearson told me the German had been executed on 31 December but how and for what reason he did not know or, it seemed, care. Well, that is what happened all those years ago and there is now no witness, no evidence that can incriminate me in any way – and what good would it do for anyone? The only trace was the cut on my stomach. And I had a look at the area the other day. There was more of it than there used to be but there is no scar now…

***

Footnote

I was interested to discover, 40 years later, in a book entitled *Battle of Britain Then and Now* published by Battle of Britain Prints International Ltd, New Plaistow Road, London East 15 3JA and, I believe, edited by Winston Ramsey, the following entry (quoted as-is – admittedly it includes many abbreviations but I think you'll get the gist):

Sunday, 15 September 1940
9 Staffel, Kampfgeschwader 2 (9/KG 2)
DORNIER Do 17z (Serial 3405) shot down by P/O Patullo of 46 Sq. during operational sortie to bomb London. Crashed in sea of Herne Bay. 3.30pm
Crew: Uffz Hoppe & Oberfhr. Staib killed.
Gefr. Hoffman & Gefr. Zierer captured.
Aircraft coded U5 + FT destroyed.

Something She Said

"Well, that's enough about me – nothing of interest to report over the four years since I last saw you, and that about sums up my present lifestyle. Now, what about you, what have you been doing?"

"Just a minute… You say nothing of interest – I reckon a wife, two kids, a house, a car, a motorbike, a bicycle, a pony and a dog, all gathered in four years, I reckon that is something. A hell of a lot more than I have to show. You know I left MAFESCO – the ill famed Middle and Far East Shipping Company?"

The other man gave a brief shake of his head.

"Well, I did, anyway. Through them I'd made some contacts, you see, with certain oil companies. So off I went, out to the Gulf. Moneywise, as they say, I've done fairly well, had a good time, seen a lot, been about a bit. But that's about all, Jimmy-the-one. That reminds me, the old name in the old gang. What happened to Jimmy-the-twoth?"

"Oh, he became obsessed with boats. Always going off somewhere. Last I heard, he was off to the West Indies. Funny thing about him though – I thought we called him Jimmy-the-twoth to distinguish us from each other but he once told me he was known to his family as Jimmy-the-tooth after they found he'd stuck one of his fallen out first teeth into his ear."

"Didn't know that, but it sounds just like him."

"So, Charlie boy, you haven't married?"

"No. I nearly did. Perhaps I should have done, but it was just something – something she said on a certain occasion."

"Don't tell me – she just said 'NO'."

"No, it wasn't that. Quite the opposite, actually."

"This sounds exciting. Tell me about it, unless it is a sensitive subject?"

"Well, it is really. But I have puzzled over it for so long. You might be able to make a judgement. Not that it matters, really. It's far too late."

"All right, Charlie boy. I won't rib you. What happened?"

"Well, there was this girl, Pamela. Pamela Briggs she was. A typist with MAFESCO. Just an ordinary type, to make a feeble pun. Nothing special about her, really. A bit dowdy, if you know what I mean. Nearly always had the same non-descript dress on. Not too well off, I think and at 20 years old not overpaid by the firm. I quite liked her, I guess.

Our work put us together a bit. Then, one day I moved into a two-roomed semi-basement flat in a house just behind the docks. It was a bit grim and I decided to do a bit of redecorating and a very limited bit of refurbishing. Hadn't a lot of cash to throw around, you understand. But I couldn't make my mind up about the colour scheme. The carpet that came with the tenancy, for example, was a very bright green with huge orange-coloured sunflowers all over it. The curtains were a sort of purple, with deep red vertical stripes. I couldn't afford to replace these but I could – and I intended to – do something about the peeling wallpaper which had a motif of hundreds of small birds swinging about on silver-coloured rings. But what to do? Well, I mentioned this problem to Pamela and she said she thought she could help. She could come up with some ideas if she could see the problem at first hand.

"So one day when we left work she came along with me to the little flat. I thought perhaps we could have a cup of tea and she could make a list of the sort of colours, paints and papers I could get. Then I'd be able to get the job done before the autumn. That was the theory but it didn't quite work out like that. In fact we didn't even put the kettle on or look at the horrible colours. She took off her light raincoat and stood with it in her hand wondering what to do with it. I went to take it from her and somehow – I have no idea how – we were suddenly in a tight embrace. She had, I discovered with surprise, full warm lips. And her figure, pressed tightly to me, was a heaven of feminine curves. How was it I had never noticed this before? I must've been blind.

"The coat dropped to the floor after a while and with a gradual movement that seemed like the slow motion steps of a weird foxtrot, we made our way to the divan. I don't think either of the partners in this slow motion walk was a leader or was led. I think it must have been a unanimous effort.

"We lay there for a while, captured in the ecstasy of the situation. Then my desire overcame any possible restraint. I went to remove her panties but I couldn't find the elasticated top. There wasn't one. Pamela removed her lips from mine and smiled.

"'That's not the way,' she said, 'don't you know about French knickers? There are two little buttons…'

"Not for long. The thought that this quite innocent young thing in the rather tatty office dress should be wearing pure silk cami-knickers with lace edging was too much for me…

Some time later, I was thinking of what extraordinary good fortune I had to find a mate, a wife, the only possible woman in the world for me to marry, to love, to cherish, forsaking all others for ever. I was about to tell her all this, to pop the question, as it were, and to get her to name the marriage date – the sooner the better.

"'Darling,' she said, 'I'm so glad you were the first.'"

The Lucky Man

As I walked past the old club, I was surprised to see that the ornamental coping still had a gap. My thoughts went back, back to… was it 1950? 1955? We were the only three members in the club when he came in. Although possibly not the biggest bore in London, he must have been in the top ten and there were general – but politely muted – sighs around as Terry Sheppard came over to us.

"I say, what shocking weather!" he said, "it reminds me of when I was in India – the monsoon, you know. Have I told you about the time I was…"

"Marooned in a bungalow with the CO's wife?" we chorused. "Yes, you have."

"Not that that will stop you," muttered Alec.

"Well, anyway it's really bad outside now."

Terry settled down at the table where Alec, Robert and I were seated.

"It's probably this foul weather that's kept the others away, sorts out the men from the boys, does a day like this," said Robert.

Just as we expected and feared, Terry took over the conversation. In a way, it was a relief from the world affairs we had been discussing – abortively of course – the only solution to the state of the world being, as usual, Robert's remedy which consisted mainly of shooting anyone who disagreed with him. And the number of these was many.

"You know how lucky I am," said Terry "I was halfway along Albemarle Street when the heavens opened. No coat, no umbrella and no shelter in sight, when along comes this car with a beautiful blonde and it and she draws up beside me and asks, can she help me? I tell you I didn't waste a second before popping in beside her and she dropped me off here. Going to take her to dinner tomorrow. Lucky, eh?"

"Chance," said Alec.

"Fate," said Robert.

"Coincidence," said I.

"Nonsense. I tell you it's luck." Terry sounded a bit irritable. "What about that time a couple of months ago in the flood?"

We all kept silent. With a bit of luck – for us – he, like the floods, would subside, go away, sink into the ground. Or something. Anything. But no, Terry was in a mood to continue. I looked out of the window. Rain was still bucketing down, the skies were black and angry-looking and even while I watched, a vicious, jagged streak of lightning flashed across the scene. No escape. We all seem to have reached the same decision. At any rate, we ordered another round of drinks and settle down in our chairs, resigned. He was going to do it again, talk about his blasted good luck!

"Well, it was in Worcester, near Pershore, and I was heading for the Malverns. There was this bumbling old idiot in front of me, crawling along, and I knew that if I didn't pass before the narrow bridge about a mile ahead I was going to be stuck behind him along the narrow twisting road for several miles afterwards. So when I saw my chance I stuck my thumb on the hooter button and shot past him. He gave me a furious dirty look – which I ignored. A bit further on, just before the bridge, my engine went dead. Cut right out. I didn't know what it was, but the roads were awash and I thought I might have water in the ignition system somewhere. So I pulled onto the side and switched off the engine. The fellow I just passed came splashing by with an infuriating grin on his face. He made a gesture of some sort of the drove onto the bridge. Halfway across, the bridge gave way and then suddenly he and his car toppled straight into the flooded river and disappeared from sight downstream. There was absolutely nothing I could do but return the way I'd come and give the alarm. Without thinking, I switched on the engine. The engine started immediately and I turned the car around and returned to the last village I had passed and reported what had happened. Now, how do you account for that? Don't you agree that was pure luck?"

"Not for the other bloke. Just chance," said Alec.

"Fate," said Robert.

"Coincidence," said I, "just a bit of water on the plugs, engine cuts out, you wait a few minutes and engine heat dries the plugs and off you go again."

"Nonsense," Terry was getting into his stride now. "I tell you it's just this extraordinary good luck I have. I've always had it. All the things that have happened in my favour can't be coincidence. Take that time during the war when I was a Radio Instructor at an RAF Advanced Training Station. My job was to fly with the crew of any aircraft allotted to me, on training flights and to teach and check and report on the Wireless Operator. I was climbing into the aircraft for which I was listed when Squadron Leader Perry, the senior instructor grabbed me by my ankle.

"'Who have you got up there?' he asked.

"'Jackson,' I replied.

"'Right,' he says, 'I want to see for myself how he's getting on. Not too happy about him. We'll swap over. You take Miller, in V Victor, okay?'

"Well, there was no use arguing about it so down I climbed – and up he went. 23 minutes later, that plane crashed and burned. They were all killed. Don't you agree that was pure luck?"

"Chance," said Alec but with less conviction than usual.

"Fate," said Robert, "when you've got to go, you go. It just wasn't your time."

"Coincidence," said I, but I wasn't quite sure about that. Could coincidence always favour the same person? I was beginning to believe in pure luck and I sensed that the other two were also.

Terry was quick to press the gains he obviously saw he had made.

"I could go on for hours," he started was interrupted by a chorus of "well, don't", "Oh no" and so on.

Undismayed, he looked briefly at his wristwatch.

"I've got to dash off. But I must just give you one more example, to convince you. A double one actually."

We kept quiet, possibly feeling that relief was close.

"It was when I was in the Home Guard," he started.

"Got around a bit didn't you?" – this from Alec.

"We were in the guard hut on the cliffs one evening, and one of the new recruits was practising loading and firing his short Lee Enfield rifle, using clips of five cartridges with wooden bullets – the usual practice – when a corporal came in off patrol, unloaded his rifle, which had real live ammunition, and – so we discovered later – laid the clip down on the table. The recruit picked it up in mistake for his own practice clip and shoved it in his rifle. He worked the bolts to put one up the breach and fired. There was this almighty big bang in a confined space and the bullet went through the sleeve of my tunic, grazing my chest, and out through the wooden wall of the hut – and killed the sentry who was pacing up and down outside."

"Was I lucky or not? Eh? Well, the incident kept me late, too late to get some petrol at the garage in town and my tank was showing empty. So I took a chance and in the dark I took the direct route home: about four miles of country lanes. I covered about one mile when the engine failed on a slight downward slope, so I freewheeled, thinking to get as far as possible. And there in the middle of the road was an American jerry can. Yes, it was full. About four and a half gallons of petrol. Now you really must agree that that was pure luck. Not chance, or fate or coincidence but pure luck. And having finally convinced you, I'm off."

I think we all felt a bit baffled and beaten. So much so that I said, "I've got my car around the corner and I'm giving these two a lift – come along if you like."

"Thanks a lot," said Terry, "but I'll grab a taxi – I want to go on from the flat."

"You're not likely to get a taxi in this weather," said Alec, "unless of course your good luck comes to your help again."

"We'll find out."

Terry rose to his feet and we all made our way to the entrance hall. Outside the storm still raged, the high wind driving rain in gusts before it, the lightning flashes showing dense black clouds above. The doorman opened the outer door for us.

"What is the chance of a taxi for Mr Sheppard?" asked Alex.

"Not a hope, sir. Haven't seen one go by this last half-hour."

Terry stepped forward, under the portico. And round the corner, as though on cue, came a taxi – with its "For Hire" sign lit up. Terry flagged it down.

"See what I mean? Don't want to rub it in, but that's the way it is. So long."

The doorman reached for his huge umbrella, opened and it and held it over Terry while he escorted him down the steps to the waiting cab. About three steps from the bottom, there was a terrible hissing sound and an instantaneous explosion as lightning struck the umbrella, hurling the doorman several yards away into the road, where he lay, face down in the pouring rain.

We were all shocked. Stunned. Unable to move. Except Terry. He lifted his head and seemed to say something about luck. Whatever he was going to say was blown away by the wind and he never had a chance to repeat it because rather more than a hundredweight of stone coping, no doubt torn off the roof by the lightning or the gale, crashed down on his upturned face. He was killed instantly.

It was incredibly silent after the noise of the lightning strike and the crash of the falling masonry. Not one of us moved.

And then:

"Chance," said Alec.

"Fate," said Robert.

"Coincidence," said I.

A Question of Colour

The weather was foul, even for a winter's day in England, and the loudspeaker announcement of an hour's delay on all flights came as no great surprise to the waiting passengers. They were already bored, listless and frustrated in the departure hall at the airport.

To fill in the time, I organised myself with two cups of tea and a fancy cake so grotesque in appearance that I bought it to study rather than to eat. I moved out of the queue. Looking for an empty table – have you noticed the old English habit of keeping all others at a distance as far as possible? I found the only vacant seat was one of two at a corner table. The other seat was occupied by a man whose face was hidden from view behind an ostentatiously opened *Times*.

"Do you mind?" I asked, putting my tray on the table with enough violence to show that I didn't care if he did not.

"Er, no of course not."

My table companion lowered his newspaper.

"Tony!"

"George!"

Recognition was instant, mutual, affable, surprised, reserved. We did not shake hands. I knew Tony Stretchford as a local pub acquaintance and although with such friendships many curtains are drawn aside one simply does not shake hands – certainly not until sufficient time for the acquaintanceship to ripen has passed and I had known Tony Stretchford for only three or four years. He was a traveller of sorts, selling various electronic pieces and bits with apparently very good results. He also had a fund of dubious – or worse – jokes that seem to be traditional in that trade and a large number of stories of his various amorous conquests in nearly every town in the UK. He was, however, still considered to be a likeable fellow.

"Where you off to?" he asked.

"Nowhere, unfortunately," I replied, "Just meeting some relatives – due in half an hour ago. And you?"

He hesitated before answering.

"I'm off to Africa," he said. "I'd very much like to tell you about it as I don't expect to come back and I haven't had the nerve to tell anyone. It so absurd, so frightening. You will probably only laugh at me but it doesn't matter now. I should be gone for good soon."

Slightly taken aback by this but very curious and hoping all would be explained before his flight was called, I put on a serious face and expressed my concern and interest. This is his story.

***

It was 5 November when he fell ill. He remembered it well because it was Guy Fawkes Night and also the end of the Darts league and he wasn't well enough to play in the away match at the Nag's Head. So he turned in early, shivering so much that his teeth chattered. After a while he slept fitfully, awakening about 3:30 am. About then, he thought, because the moon had gone down and his small bedroom was very faintly lit by starlight only. He felt better, cooler. He discovered that the eiderdown had slipped off the bed and he could just make out its shape. He reached out to grasp it and pull it back onto the bed but instead of the soft, silky feel of the eiderdown, what he touched was a rounded object of very course, furry hair with what felt like a small horn on each side. He let out a yell.

"What the hell???"

A well-spoken, quiet, reassuring sort of voice answered him.

"Nearly right. Certainly in the right direction. Getting warm you might say. But not HIMSELF. I'm only a Collector. A Senior Collector."

"Collector of what?"

Tony was surprised to find himself quite cool and calm. His initial shock had worn off very quickly.

"Why, Collector of Souls of course," said the Collector. "Surely you must have thought about it? What do you think happens to your soul when collection time comes? You must have realised that WE and THE OTHER ONES are dependent on souls from earth for our power? We aren't interested in your earthly forms – no one is. Their growth maintenance and expiry are, of course, completely random things. The soul comes to US inevitably. It's only a question of who gets what. When you have a war or open a new motorway, it merely means a good harvest to us. That's why I'm talking to you, against the rules. Your Soul Collection warning light was orange which means that we would have had to use the SVM. I say, 'would have' because your light has faded away so there will be no collection tonight."

"SVM?" Said Tony, "what the devil is that?"

"There is no need to be blasphemous," said the Collector. "The SVM is the SOUL VIBRATION METER."

He had this strange ability to speak in capital letters when he felt it necessary.

"I see you do not understand. So, as we've got this far – and I'm sure you will be one of ours when the time comes – I'll explain. Very roughly, of course. You see, when your soul is ready for collection, it gives off a light. That is how we collectors know when to call. If the soul is for us, it has a red light. If it belongs to the OTHER ONES, it has a yellow light. Now, yours was a most unusual one, being orange coloured it could have belonged to either side. So careful measurement would have been necessary to decide whether it was more red than yellow or the other way round. As it is faded away, it doesn't arise now and anyway I'm satisfied that it was mainly red and that you belong to US."

"You mean," said Tony, still amazed at his own calmness, "that what we do in life affects the colour of our souls and therefore where it goes?"

"Exactly," said the Collector.

"And now I must go myself. I spent too much time with you as it is. Very interesting, though. We don't get many exactly orange ones and very rarely one that fades. See you again soon."

There was a terribly strong smell, reminiscent of fireworks or the chemistry lab at school. Tony put out his hand where the Collector had been and again let out a loud yell. He had burned his hand and the room seemed full of smoke. There was a loud peremptory knocking on the door, following by the rattling of the door handle, which, Tony said, had always been very loose. The light went on and his housekeeper was in the room.

"Mr Stretchford, what is going on?" she demanded.

Measured about the chest – or the seat – she was about the same as her height and in a dressing gown of blue, decorated with large purple flowers she presented an awesome sight. At least Tony thought so, for his reply was confused and incoherent mainly to the effect that he didn't know what was going on.

"You don't know?" bellowed Miss Kirby in a voice that could easily have controlled a parade ground.

"Then I'll make a guess. You've dropped a lighted cigarette, fallen asleep, drunk no doubt, and burnt the eiderdown and the carpet. I'll not stay here to be burnt to death in my bed by such goings-on. I've looked after you for a long time but really, this is too much."

Tony felt the amazed outrage of someone wrongly accused.

"You know I don't smoke," he said angrily, "and I was ill when I turned in, not drunk and I don't know what's happened any more than you."

Oh God, he thought suddenly, yes I do but I can't possibly say it.

"Well," boomed Miss Kirby, "if it's not a cigarette end it's fireworks you've been playing with. Or explosives. I know that smell – it's sulphur. You can't fool me." She glared at Tony as though convinced he belonged to the IRA or something unspeakably worse. In spite of her brusque attitude it was clear that she was frightened.

Tony was about to deny this firework charge when it occurred to him that the carpet *was* scorched and the eiderdown *was* burnt and how the devil could he explain it? He winced inwardly at his own choice of words.

"Well," he said, "I did have this firework. For indoor use, it said. I didn't know it would go off like that."

"Oh well," said Miss Kirby, calming down a bit, "the expense of a new eiderdown and carpet these days will make you think twice before being so silly again. I'll see to it in the morning. Meanwhile I'll make your cup of tea downstairs while the smoke and smell clear out of here." She flung open the window and marched off, her heavy tread on the stairs expressing strong disapproval of whatever it was going on.

"And so," said Tony to me, "that is what happened. And that's why I've sold my house, left my job and I'm off to Africa. I've joined the mid-African Pentecostal coastal missionaries and I shall work with them until I've picked up a bit of yellow colouring."

At that moment the loudspeaker sprang to life and called for all passengers with boarding passes for flight 113 for African airports to go to gate number three.

Tony stood up, held out his hand, which I shook and he departed.

"You'd better think about it too…" he said, over his shoulder. I did not say a word. But I'm still thinking about it.

About the Author

Clive Lodge was born in 1909. He joined the RAF voluntarily during the Second World War, serving mainly as a navigator with the rank of flight lieutenant. He usually flew Beaufighters – on night-fighting missions - but like many people he always had a deep affection for the Spitfire.

Immediately after the war he was sent to India as an Intelligence Officer to investigate the causes of crashes by planes returning British troops home.

After leaving the RAF, Clive worked in banking for many years but his twin preoccupations were inventions – he won medals for his fog lamp and his cloches designs – and boats – he and a couple of friends set up a boat yard in Lymington, Hampshire, making power boats.

Always active, at seventy, he fell out of an oak tree, electric saw in hand. Amazingly he survived the fall.

Clive Lodge died in 1983.

About the Editor

Lesley Lodge, daughter of Clive Lodge, is an eclectic writer – horses in film, historical crime and housing finance. To see her books or for more information you can visit her website at: www.lesleylodge.co.uk

Night Mission Beer

2014 – the year I discovered my Dad's stories in the loft – was also the year I found Night Mission Beer.

Night Mission Beer is a gluten-free beer that actually tastes like beer. It's made by Glebe Farm in Cambridgeshire, in the UK. Glebe Farm's owners explain that the name 'Night Mission' came about because of the farm's historical links to the famous wartime pathfinder squadrons. The Pathfinder Force consisted of Mosquitos and Lancasters, flown by the most experienced aircrew who dropped flairs with great accuracy on the night's target as markers for the bomber crews that followed. The Pathfinder Force won several Victoria Crosses but suffered many losses. Their contribution to the war effort is said to have helped shorten the duration of World War II.

There were several Pathfinder airfields in the area of Glebe Farm - the farm was next to RAF Wyton, the wartime HQ of the Pathfinder. Remnants of crashed aircraft have been found in Glebe farm fields! Night Mission beer bottle labels show a World War II Mosquito aircraft. It was a pathfinder Mosquito that crashed into the fields at Glebe Farm while attempting to land at its base, RAF Wyton.

Printed in Great Britain
by Amazon